LOCAL AUTHOR DATE DUE   OCT 0 5

GAYLORD			PRINTED IN U.S.A.

AND THE STARS GAVE US NAMES

POEMS

Joyce Epstein
Patricia Parish Kuhn
Sara Jameson

ACKNOWLEDGMENTS

JOYCE EPSTEIN
"Battlefield Dreams" was published in the chapbook, *A Journey Through Life Unguarded*. "Mother Owed Me Memories" and "Journey" appeared previously in *West Wind Review*; "Mother Owed Me Memories" was also performed by the Theatre Arts Departments of Southern Oregon State College and the University of Portland. "Re-Discovery" was the winner of an Oregon State Poetry Association Award in 1995.

SARA JAMESON
"At the Poetry Reading" appeared previously in the 1996 *Rogue's Gallery*. "Skyball" appeared previously in the *Grants Pass Daily Courier*. "Blood Is Thicker" was the winner of an Oregon State Poetry Association Award in 1995. "Celestial Navigation" won a first place award from the Oregon State Poetry Association in 1996.

PATRICIA PARISH KUHN
"Rape of a Virgin" appeared previously in *West Wind Review* 1992 and was performed by the Drama Departments of Southern Oregon State College and the University of Portland. "Artemis Strikes" appeared previously in *Hesperides*. "Quiet Conversation" appeared previously in *Southern Oregon Currents*. "Seascape" was the winner of an Oregon State Poetry Association Award in 1996. "wayne" appeared previously in *West Wind Review*.

Library of Congress Catalog Card Number
96-90841

Joyce Epstein, Patricia Parish Kuhn, Sara Jameson
    And the Stars Gave Us Names

First edition

ISBN: 0-9647066-2-8

Printed in the United States of America

Wellstone Press

A Trillium Book
P.O. Box 3565, Ashland, Oregon 97520

*Truth enters the mind so easily
that when we hear it for the first time
it seems as if we were simply
recalling it to memory.*

—Bernard de Fontenelle, 1708

CONTENTS

JOYCE EPSTEIN

SARA JAMESON

PATRICIA PARISH KUHN

JOYCE EPSTEIN

STONES OF SILENCE

Walking on stones of silence she was
brave, taking the chance of slipping
on the round gray surfaces
worn smooth by
surf pounding upon sand, upon itself
where time has walked this way,
a path of limited endurance
where distance is measured privately,
and shades of meaning
fall between stones.

She numbered her footfalls
like counting sheep, as night
dropped its curtain across the stage.
Out of step in the darkness,
feet tripping over themselves,
she tried to balance yes and no,
left essays hanging in mid-air,
she struggled on.
But she was brave
alone, in the dark
and as the silence deepened,
the stones came to life. They sang
of heroines, while
the stars of Orion's belt
showed her the way again
and the sirens sang.

THE PIANO

Among earliest memories
     after the war
my piano still remains
     in a quiet corner of my room,
keys soft under my fingers
     the reality of small hands
          that never
               reached
                    an octave
But in dreams the ivories
     were like ripening virgins,
harmony spread over the keys
     in a lover's caress, rich
melodies of woven innocence

Legato woman now
     with the yellowing
of ivories, the piano's felts
     dried out and mostly out of
tune, but the fantasies
     remain, a timeless metronome,
     deepening
          the rhythms
               of my life.

THE AGE OF ANXIETY

At twenty she counted
     seven-thousand three hundred
days and nights stored in her mind's
     warehouse, seeping through surfaces
of skin hidden from reality by rouge
     and red lips, the effect of which
though well-intentioned, foiled
     libido, lover, kin, awakened
longing, lame excuses for not
     being perfect. She was good at
games and politics, a twentieth
     century mind turning over pages
for enlightenment. Meeting this
     woman in an age of anxiety
seven thousand three hundred
     days and nights later, at forty
rouge gone, lips bolder now,
     her words tightened around
her curve of the world. Her
     breath was free but in making
sense of neutrons and spiders,
     what may have separated us
was the ring on my finger.

I AM MARKED BY SHARPENED SILENCES

I am marked by sharpened silences.
I go to synagogue on Friday nights
once a month, uncommitted
but not impious, looking
for my connection to
five thousand years,
some bridge over rivers
of understanding.

The going is important, is
the connection to the synagogue,
a play on words, a sin-agog where
words by rote unite the congregants,
the synagogue as stage for worship,
stage for change.

I learn the songs by rote, their
cadences connect my mind
to different levels of time and being,
measures of devotion, relevant
to my place in the universe,
in my small neighborhood
of reverence.

Say *adonai*, there is in *adonai*
a nourishment of meaning, a richness
in the sound of my intonement.
I sound the word *kodesh*, repeat the
word *kodesh kodesh kodesh* until
I own it now.

The now when I am there
is not in conflict with a need

for deeper understanding, scientific
reference. I close my eyes when
saying the *shema*, I alter nothing,
hear only the distances of history.

If my devotion lacks engagement
it is the force of others whose devotion
challenges my intellect and sense
of moral obligation. Although
we often drink from similar
cups of understanding, it is within
I alter my reflection, the sound of words,
as I am marked by sharpened silences.

COMING IN THIRD

In billowing white clouds
between green mountains
on the edge of a Pacific
night, an unmanned
Japanese satellite,
blasts off
as snow falls gently
on the rocket's slender
skin, and the winds
that blow spread Saka-
jurima's living volcanic
ash in innocent
gesture on the nestled
launch of a lunar probe.
A race already won
among the monitors, mass
readouts by the engineers,
science of a nation's
imprisoned soul,
mechanical witchcraft
on the front line
of a social masquerade.
And while the wind
blows live in the eyes
of history, do they
write haiku on the moon

when the moon is over
Kyoto and the moon
over Kyoto is the
same one I see through
the window panes
of the world
blowing itself
to pieces where
the people always
come in third.

January, 1990

RETREAT IN WINTER

In my simple landscape of lofty conifers
an old deodar cedar spreads its branches
beyond its lawnbed of brown needles, while

across a neighbor's fence a white fir grows
seeming out of place in low country.
It is this tiny forest I take for granted.

Were I in wilder wood, hearing the thunder
of felled trees, I would gather Greek
choruses to mourn and their sound

would echo in the world's forests.
I would dwell in a house of straw,
release my poems from paper's bondage.

Instead, in the distilled wetness of morning
I retreat to my winter landscape
in the soft needles of widow's weeds,
          asking for forgiveness.

THOUGHTBOXES/MINDBOXES

Everyone laughed
at Robert Rauschenberg's
thoughtboxes
in Rome
at the Galleria
dell'Obelisco.
I hid in the
corner with
my mindboxes,
mixing metaphors,
assembling words
in mid-air, not hearing
their laughter.
I spoke at last,
a brave warrior.
Art is a
gambol, I said,
a frolic on a
cool river
that empties
into an ocean
of surprises.
Art is a
gamble, he said,
throwing the
dice in mid-
air, laughing,
coming close
to me, touching
me, telling me
love doesn't
exist in Rome.

BURYING GUILT

Layered echoes of earth
resonate across half a century
to summers of innocence
a country life she wasn't born to,
where her grandfather
divined lawns and flower beds,
and whose salads were festooned
with the sweet meat of his moist-
ripened tomatoes and ruffled greens.

Surveying the scene now
across her own backyard
three thousand miles
from yesterday,
thatches of dry devilgrass
and yellow bursts of dandelion
battle for position where lush fescue
long ago surrendered; a frilly
rhododendron hugs the siding
for comfort, its blossoms stillborn;
fending for itself, only a prize-winning
rose flourishes: *Peace,* a goodwill gesture
in beds long ago taken over
by St. John's Wort.

Enriched by the fertile
loam of history, a city-bred
woman tries to bury her guilt
in the fresh soil of deeply urban roots.

JOURNEY

A travelogue
hastily put together
takes us through life unguarded,
while narrators
color the grey grass green
and tell us
the people are not starving.

The nightmare of the night before,
I try to tell you
the train no longer
stops here, the seats are taken,
every inch of space is spoken for.

The journey is about to end,
an aborted itinerary
in my pocket
along with a passport
to the tomb of the unknown soldier
who weeps for the ticket taker
at each station.

MY FATHER WAS A NICE MAN

In the gleaming white Buick
my father bought for Sunday rides
in the country,
there was always room
for one more in the car:
widowed aunts, friends,
strangers if they needed it.
Smart man that he was
some still took advantage;
he trusted business partners,
should have known better,
but he was much too nice.
And nice today

      is not how you get to the moon
or be a union organizer,
even president of a company.
But those were not
my father's aspirations.
He liked to gamble a little,
play pinochle with his cronies,
figure out a good horse
in the seventh at Belmont,
sit down with the evening paper
to work word games
as I straddled his armchair.

      I look upon his innocence
with city-bred sophistication;
but then neither
was my father innocent
in the good old days when boys

became men too quickly
and ward politics in the big city
the orphanage for small believers.

Yet he blushed easily
at off-color jokes, heat rushing up
from round cheeks to balding crown
where he combed the last few hairs
of his manliness.
He wore nice honorably
along with other ribbons
for fidelity and veracity.

I'm not yet comfortable with his death,
saved his grey suede shoes in a trunk
for twenty years, still waiting
for history to repeat itself
so I could write a different finish
to this story

      but as beneficiary
I can only color or invent
the truth or half-truths
of this simple man
as metaphors grow stale
in a store-front
of disentangled memories.

WHEN IS A POEM NOT ENOUGH

when is a poem not enough?
when pain and memory
tighten breath like a house
closed up for summer,
when escape is no longer
in language, familiar quotations
no longer companions
to alleviate suffering

can we expect a poem to
release forgiveness
when residues of guilt remain
serviced by words
that twist like screws
into the heart of matter

or can a poem float downstream
in a shallow river
where words
like stones of sorrow
lie naked,
where sunlight
tipples the water like angel dust
and dandelions
might even grow on the riverbank,
small miracles in the
passage of mourning

UPHEAVAL

in the pre-dawn cold as gods
shivered in the layered violence
a wake for victims,
for trees, houses,
fences straddled between strangers

how many were making love
at four-thirty in the morning,
how many were deeply involved
on the darker side of the moon,
and how many would be hostages
in the aftermath, broken lives
broken glass in the shattered
landscape of a fifteen second
nightmare

and in the crash of crystal
who could detect the belltones
of Tiffany or Waterford

and in the aftermath
who would sing the lullabies

A FRAGMENTARY LIFE

In small town newspapers
some stories get only a line or two.
It takes few lines
to deliver pain.
Sylvia Plath's suicide
might only have made page eleven,
if at all.

Plath had company.
Other poets bear such pain:
the uneasy charge of words
that choke and clog the veins
where hearts burn, seared by
missed meanings.

For how many is poetry
surely death,
a tryst with the devil,
at best, long sleep,
a walk on the moors
as critics draw conclusions.

Cures are available
but slow surrender,
that carcinoma of control,
marks the metered journey:
the short gestation period
of a poet's suicide.

LIFE AS ADVENTURE

life as adventure
turns inside out
like a reversible
jacket

no wasted dreams:
you survive
by reinventing
yourself
and time

even in snow storms
you find your way out,
even with strangers
who believe
all the stories
are theirs

winter's worry
slips on the icy parade
of its victims

a man in a furred hat
turns his face to the wind
and drinks the snowflakes
like fine wine
his footfalls silent proof
that he had
walked this way

THE QUIET STAR

there was a star   one star in
the new universe   it was the so-called
quiet star   I read about it
in yesterday's evening paper   opened
to page 3   amid other stories
one life saved   another abandoned
grieving   faceless images
and I stood   there in the kitchen
now holding a book at   arm's
length   due at the library
three days ago   lost
under another evening paper
I look for other   ways to lose self
a Mozart piano concerto   lifts me
amid the miracles to believe
in God   but I have more train rides
to take   in order to believe
when the holiest of days comes
it's all   written in a book
published yearly   who will live and
who will not survive and
there I   stood in the kitchen
reading the holocaust poems
and I began   to cry the crying
came softly like the quiet star
I had read about on page 3 in
yesterday's but you know that
the room was warm   ninety outside
I had toasted   English muffins and

stood there in the kitchen
reading Yevtushenko
out loud   and Philip Levine and
Denise Levertov I know and other poets
unfamiliar names   but they were not
nameless   like the victims
of the fires   or of the gasses with
distinguishing characteristics
rising   in the ashes
of remembrance
stripped of their
humanity   raw   uneducated phosphorus
calcereous tissue was   all that
remained some buried and the poets
they all   knew
some how
a voice like a
quiet star

ALDONADO

Fleshtones glisten under the kitchen's
blue fluorescent light as he glides orders
smoothly over the stainless steel counters

as I, staring at the curve of his neck where it
nuzzles his ear, there behind the sizzling grill, he,
leaning, bending over and under, a man

who witnesses the night, who knows his power
as I fill my gut watching his skin glisten
under the kitchen's blue fluorescent light

where I watch him wipe the sweat from his brow
with a white cloth napkin and suddenly he
sees me watching and his black eyes know me

and the stainless steel glistens

and I am no longer recognizable

RE-DISCOVERY

Inland in Ashland you forget about the sea,
the Siskiyous lulling you into a different horizon
dense, green, ascending, vulnerable.
Missing the sea
I set out on an overcast day seeking
treasures buried in the shifting sands of childhood,

along the way skirting forest where
rhododendron wrap gracefully around
eight hundred year old redwoods, their blossoms
bred in pine-needle blankets,
a quiet lagoon, artery
to the sea's heart, where migratory waterfowl
refresh, encode their destination,
where forest floor gives way to carpets
of sand and stone.

A rush of sea air swept me
forward, seafoam soon to clothe me, its pull
never owning its own pulse,
while the distant fog bank
hung in its own haze, waiting for a chance
to envelop the still morning air.

The nearness
of the mist moistened my lips.
In that cool salubrious moment at water's edge,
the taste of salt in a final embrace.

OVERDUE NOTICES

       arrived from
early missionaries,
their catechisms
like quivers of love,
their tongues
tasting of salt
like the margaritas
served at the Algonquin Hotel
in mid-town Manhattan
that replaced the carbonated
soft drinks of innocence,

       mentors
of an artist's life,
the politics of change,
views of the world
separating lullabies
from blues
as she fled
into the arms

       of Robinson Jeffers
and Pablo Neruda,
forever James Joyce,
Brahms and Alben Berg
Goya
Picasso
Georgia O'Keefe

Maimonides,
Mencken, muckrakers
and union organizers:
those were gifts, prizes
collected in her anteroom,
like lovers whose kisses
remain under the threadbare
fabric of memory.

MOTHER OWED ME MEMORIES

Mother owed me memories
leaving the earth, my ground
speechless, unafraid
no last breath waiting to be heard;
unaware of my longing
for her life stories, mysteries of birth,
her own, the history of all
before, her sins, small glories.

Coy she was, no Jewish princess
but kept her thinning hair
touched up with henna rinses,
always laughed at my father's jokes
stepping on her own,
still reached up
to move hair off my face at forty
as she did when I was five,
and ten, and twenty.
Dying as she did, a yellow rose
that I had tucked into her hair,
fair skin fooling all of us,
she left this world and I am
trying to forgive her now.

BATTLEFIELD DREAMS

Flaming tongues of war
Lick the ruins of the larger world
As soldiers of fortune in an arms race
Build their dirty bridges behind them,
Burying the people, burying the children
Who plea for nothing but life in the ashes,
There in the ruins of false hope,
Dreaming in colors
Only the blind can see.

And when morning comes
Quickened by the stench of death,
Who will look for the sun
On the beach, in the sand?
Who will see the wounded
As the generals close ranks.

Genocide, small wars, revolts,
Will occupy at most
A page or two of history.
Flowers will be thrown on every grave.
Daisies.
Chrysanthemums.
As falling stars hesitate
Before landing in the ruins,
I hide in the guilt of night's survival
Dreaming of a flock of white doves.

LOVE IS WHAT YOU MAKE OF IT

As a country, are we bereft
because we have no pageantry, because
our history seems made up like fairytales,
some of which leave us unafraid, others
that scare us into believing we need
love to make it better?

In England, monarchy is tested every
day in the London Times,
while the dons of Oxford have
neither answers
nor do they trifle with the people's faith;
the stones of each cathedral
bear the burdens of confession,
buried bones in catafalques, pall-covered coffins
filled with history's secrets,
philosophers' uncertainties.

Our anthems are not young,
but legends lie discarded, wasted
in the stillness of quiet promises of heaven.
Dreams are held for ransom
as hostages parade before our eyes in cadence:
smoothly sanded wooden soldiers
on long red carpets to whom we
doff our hats out of habit
holding ourselves as witness
to the tapestry of time.

SARA JAMESON

MOON HUNTER

The sickle moon
hangs like a silver boomerang
in the hand of the mighty Orion.
Forsaking his bow,
he draws back slow and steady
the crystal arc, sharper
than well-tempered (white-hot)
ice cold steel,
squares his shoulders —
the paired stars
Beetelgeuse and Bellatrix —
aims at the red Aldeb-
aran eye of nearby Taurus
and lets fly.

His weapon whirls across the sky,
watched by dazzling flocks of birdstars
while Orion strides behind.
And when, centuries hence,
the crescent circles back
for a catch, hunter and moon
will find themselves
together again
for another throw.

BREAKFAST MEDITATIONS

A galaxy of deep blue
berries cascades over
a golden heaven of cereal
flakes, afloat in an ocean
of milk. And I stop
swallowing absentmindedly,
look up from my book,
and think of the
real sea they sailed
from their south Pacific
New Zealand hillside
to my foggy Oregon kitchen.
Suddenly I savor the astonishing
taste of time travel.
A hint of fierce
Maori warriors dances on my tongue
as my spoon herds the soft berries
like a flock of wooly blue sheep,
whose plaintive cries echo
across those distant emerald lawns
where homesick Brits in straw boaters
play cricket and sip Chinese tea
so far from home.

LUNCH WITH MOM AT 82

I sit with you,
and spoon-feed cottage cheese
with fruit —
grapes, bananas, blueberries
red, white and blue —
just days before
the Glorious Fourth.

Sometimes you open wide
like a baby bird,
take spoon and all.
And then you chew
with slow deliberation, half-asleep,
regarding each new bite
suspiciously.

I sweet-
talk as you must have done
to me so many years ago.
"Ready for more?" I say,
holding my mouth open
the same way mothers do
though I have no baby
but you.

KISSING THE SKY

Kissing the sky goodnight,
the sun departs,
leaving a smudge of lipstick,
tonight bright salmon,
pink yesterday, tomorrow rose.

My mother would exclaim,
How lovely,
but I,
a snotty 12-year old,
would sigh. Oh Mom, I'd say,
and roll my eyes, and squirm
at her sincerity,
while secretly I also ached
with sadness
at the beauty.

It's been years now since
my mother's kisses
left their scarlet marks
upon my cheek,
the signs of love I rubbed
away, embarrassed.

Now I'm the one who cries
at loveliness. I hold her hand
and whisper, this October sky has turned
me into her. My bare lips
brush her aged face without a trace.

She cannot answer,
does not turn her greying head,
but sees, I think, the golden glow
reflected in my eyes.

JUNE 1912:
MY FATHER LEARNS ABOUT MORTALITY

You have to give me one,
says the small boy,
pointing at the fresh-made
sugar doughnuts
whose spicy smell
warms the cottage kitchen,
mixing with the sharp-scented
cool June air
of the piney Maine woods
and the salty smell of the sea
coming upriver on the tide.

You have to,
he says again
to the young black woman
brought to this alien north
to cook all summer.

I don't have to do anything but die,
she says
and turns away.

Stunned and empty-handed
the boy stumbles to the porch
letting the screen door slam sharp
against the silence,
sinks to the top step
and thinks
for the first time
about death.

IMMORTALITY

The ink bleeds
each letter swells
like a pregnant belly
grows a new life
creates a destiny
on the infinite white
future
indelibly making
its mark
for eternity

and in eternity
as the pages fade
grow brittle with age
the words will wash away
slowly become indistinct
yet a trace of life remains
a stain
immutable

SOLID AS A ROCK

I like better
a poem with concrete images
even if the concrete has been traced
with shape-shifting cloud patterns
        as it dried.
Still, that is something one can place
a hand on, something with more weight
than vaporous verse
which leaves a gritty aftertaste
        like London fogs.
And even motes of dust that dance
a lovely golden shower in the sun,
are still but insubstantial atoms.

I want a poem I can feel.

Like a drowning man
who hugs a tree,
grateful for its rough
security, or my old Ma
who grips her chair
to keep from slipping
into night,
I grasp for something solid
I can hold, else I must pinch
myself, the way she does,
to know I'm really there.

FOR JACK

My brother called today to say
his heart had only one artery,
though it forked
in two, of course,
and I wondered if
that was why he always seemed
so shy,
because the love could not get out.

He always loved me, in his way.
I've been told that at 16
he said, "I've boiled my hands.
Now can I hold the baby?"
When I was three he called me
Piggy-First Class (that made me mad)
while fixing Sunday scrambled eggs.

If I pestered him too much,
he'd say, "Let's play
building and loan.
Go out of the building and
leave me alone."
I never did.

Instead I studied
his fishing tackle, tangled lines, admired
the bamboo rod wound tight with thread
red, yellow, black, and asked
"What's this?"
"A wing-wang for a goose's bridle,"
he'd say.
And I believed him.

He took me fishing
when I turned five.
We sat beside the big rocks
under Chain Bridge where kayakers
drown each spring in the Potomac's runoff.
I caught a catfish
and we ate saltines from the pocket
of my seagreen corduroy coat.

Then he was gone.
Off to college, the Navy,
a wife, two kids.
He helped me get a summer job
at the museum where he worked.
For 30 years we spoke politely
until our father died.

Now he calls 3000 miles to talk
about his girlfriend and his cat
and what he's doing in retirement,
still shy but fond, still getting by
on one artery
that branches into two.

MY SOLITUDE CRACKS

I sit in a circle
of golden light,
before sunrise
reading transfixed
a book of poetry
that puts me in
another world.

I am content
to hear the rain,
the fire crackling,
the cat purring,
and even the refrigerator
humming.

But when I hear
your morning steps
echo down the hall
the spell is broken.

I try to be cheerful
as my solitude cracks
like a crab shell,
the delicate pink flesh
trembling inside.

TEA FOR TWO

The tray arrives.
Cozy under thick red
quilted silk,
embroidered with Chinese dragons,
and looking like a jolly
Russian grandmother,
the teapot with its snowflake sides
breathes spicy scents into the air.

We pour out comfort
into matching cups,
though no two snowflakes
are alike,
but soul mates, as we are,
the left and right sides
balancing our talk.

Silver spoons stir sweetness
and the milk of human kindness,
while forks taste the tangy
lemon bars and tart
raspberry jam that counterpoint
our honeyed words.

AT THE POETRY READING

One woman clutches
a hanky, waves it defiantly
aloft, no white flag of surrender
to middle age, but her hard-won
banner, and says
she always vowed
she wouldn't be like
her mother, but she is,
and now
she reads a poem about her
childhood, and the
blood-red kitchen
ceiling that hung
over pictures of Jesus
and the mountains
of spaghetti her mother cooked,
the poem's sweet-scented words
as warm as the smells she remembers
rising from the shiny silver stove.

In cropped red curls
and studded leather vest
another woman stands
and reads about
a very different mother/
daughter time,
not cooking together
but looking for God
in every church
in San Francisco,
and finding Him once
among the Holy Rollers,

a funny sad prophetic
scene, seen through
a teenage daughter's eyes.

One mother
was a trophy
fisherman like Hemingway
in Florida, who praised her
poet daughter more
for catching fish.

Our host reads a poignant poem
about a cherished antique aunt,
and another about his
mother whose love was twisted.
Strong stuff.

Strong women
and weak, these mothers,
whose ghosts circle round,
called up by spells of memory
at this poetry reading.

ROGUE RIBBONS

Ruffled grey ribbon
of river
edged with white foam
a watered silk
in wavy baroque folds
running full, voluptuous
beside the barren grey
asphalt ribbon
of highway
its anemic twin
hard and cold
heading straight to the point
without a single sideways glance
at its softer sister
flowing by
under a dusky veil
of mist and rain.

THE UMPQUA HILLS

The hills lie down beside the stream
in hazy summer heat
like tired cattle, dusty brown.
Along their narrow backs
a rocky skeleton protrudes;
Their scruffy coats of golden grass
are spotted white with daisies.
And tucked among their lean
and bony flanks, worn hooves
crop out through ragged fur.
Dark muzzles nestle
in a clump of trees
and breathe in gratefully
the faint green moisture
of the lingering summer stream.
And circling slowly overhead
like flies
around these antique beasts,
two lazy crows.

PETROGLYPHS

Dark spirits stand
at attention
a ragged row of rocks,
white numbers chalked
on shoulders,
stand forlorn
behind an iron fence
along a concrete wall
under Celilo Dam,
prisoners saved
from the dam's false lake
far from their birthplace
on Columbia's shore.

A life sentence.

Thousands of years
they lived beside the river.
Thirty-five years
here at the dam
with no hope
of pardon.

Ancient spirits
carved in stone
lined up against the wall
as for a firing squad
shackled to the ground
as if they might run home,

As if they were too powerful
and must be locked
up on display,
to show the power
of engineers who
domineered the river,
men who praise themselves
for stealing these few rocks
as if that would preserve
a culture lost
when the dam
destroyed the falls
doomed the villages
killed the fish
and drowned the spirits
of the people.

FADED MEMORIES HAUNT THE NIGHT

Gone grey
like a television screen at midnight
its erratic pattern, snowlike
though not soft,
not quiet, comforting,
instead
a static racket hums
disconsolately,
all meaning lost;

like an old blackboard
erased too many times,
the dusty felt smudging words
leaves only traces, ghost lines
behind.

Her memory
has become a wasteland
of dementia or maybe stroke, who knows
what, or when, or why. Her clouded eyes
look troubled, faded grey
like blue jeans washed too often.

My memories too
have faded, hazy now
my memories of her
of 20 years ago,
laughing, whacking a tennis ball
with glee, dancing a polka,
making brownies with the Girl Scouts,
and cupcakes
for my fourth grade birthday,

or sweet-tart Lime Light pie
that summer night when I flew home,
so sick I couldn't eat,
the city heat oppressive.
Her image shimmers in mirage,
dissolves
into the heavy humid air
where memories wait
to haunt the night.

EELS

Tiny currents of air
swirl round your ankles
like eels, bite through
your socks, and set
the cat's ball dangling
on a string to swaying.
You can hardly see it move
but you feel the eels.

Or is it just the earth's
turn that swings the ball,
that swirls the water
down your drain,

that sails your house a thousand
thousand miles through space,
a dizzying race through time,
your house hurtling past stars
dwarfed by constellations,

dwarfed even by the one ton squid
found off New Zealand yesterday,
twenty-six feet long, as big
as your house, as ancient
as the stars,
caught swimming through an ocean universe
through currents that circle like eels
like breaths of air
round your ankles.

SPRING

It's just the fresh light yellow
scent from a bunch of daffodils
massed in a fat glass bowl atop a
pedestal, creeping into the cool
empty corners of the art gallery
and up to the high white ceiling.

It's just the patch of ragged March
sky seen at the tiny window, scraps
of blue in a pile of grey clouds,
passing free behind the white iron
bars behind the bare black branches
of the oak.

It's just a thin line of tulips,
stiff with sorrow, swaying in the
April air beside the door.
Scarlet petals scatter
on the path, spatter like drops
of blood.
       Spring is the worst
time to die.

BLOOD IS THICKER

One by one I put them in my mouth,
black cherries, blushed burgundy,
like beautiful purple bruises.
My teeth tear their soft skin,
my tongue crushes their tender flesh,
laps up the sweet warm juice which
tastes of summer sun.

One by one a pound of these ruby
jewels slides seductively
down my thirsty throat.
Reluctantly I make
my greedy fingers stop,
cover the painted bowl and put
it back, to save some summer for
tomorrow.

One by one my grandmother
once ate an entire flat of
famous Hood River cherries,
sitting stoutly in her red summer dress
on the weedy gravel shoulder
beside the hot highway
at the Oregon border,
when the Ag inspector wouldn't
let her bring them into
California.

I can see her clearly,
this fierce woman I never met,
whose veins like mine
run red with cherry juice.

GREEN APPLES

I sit alone
peeling tart green apples,
my fingers
turning black,
stained by the juice
and the iron knife,
blisters rising
as I slice twenty pounds
into bite-sized pieces.
They bubble softly
in the quiet kitchen
with raisins, cinnamon, brown
sugar, only burning
a little in the big roasting
pan. I stir up tiny blackened
bits. Only I
will eat this applesauce.

My mother used to tell me
how she and her sister
sat at the big round kitchen table
as their mother peeled
tart green apples
with an iron knife,
her fingers stained and blistered,
scolding her children
who ate the slices
fast as she could cut them.

Year after year
my mother ate
tart green apples

which my father brought
with her morning coffee.

I was the one who made pie.

Grandmother died
before I met her,
the house sold,
the big round table gone.

Now mother has gone too,
on the long journey toward death,
and only the tart green apples remain
year after year.

CELESTIAL NAVIGATION

Each spring my field becomes
a rainbow universe.
Dazzling northern lights
dance at noon, while sunflowers
return as faithfully as Haley's comet
on a shorter cycle.
Galaxies of purple vetch
chest high to a deer,
stretch to the fence;
golden poppies shine,
a thousand thousand suns,
while lavender brodeia explodes,
a supernova on a slender stalk.
Across the acre arcs a Milky Way.
Heavenly blue chicory
fades to violet dying giants.
Daisies radiate white light
beside the drive in clever constellations.
Masses of tiny pink asteroids
spin through space,
orbiting the fixed point
of our satellite dish;
while the apple tree,
lost in a stellar cloud
of opalescent apple blossom moons,
makes navigation possible.

SKYBALL

Fat yellow ball,
that gibbous moon,
drifts slowly
down
the sky,
aiming for
the firtree goal posts
it cannot miss.

The score is certain
in this cosmic game.

PATRICIA PARISH KUHN

ODE TO A CYCLAMEN
(for Marta)

White butterfly wings
in silent dance
alight
on slender green pedestals
to honor the Goddess of the Garden.

ARTEMIS STRIKES

with her arrow poised
   the huntress goddess lets go.

unwary eyes cloud
   stunned.
   delicate fingers flee upward
   too late for moat against insensitive eyes.

cherry blossom skin
   awash with a heart's torrent,
   tumultuous heaving,
              unconsolable.

a translation gone awry?
   an ambush by a prideful, wounded goddess?
          stillness
          sleep. . .

the morrow

flight

will she come
can she come
will she forgive

impenetrable island
   from centuries of discipline
   isolation
   cultural imprinting

no match for expansive,
emotionally charged Artemis.

did the arrow sever artery of friendship?

laughter
delicate Spring beauty
                    in Shinjuku Gyoen

tears darken to blood
silken cherry blossoms
                    ground in mud

          rains come.

THE EMPEROR'S GARDEN

Silk-skinned
cherry blossom
springs forth
            from gnarled
                    ancient limb
dances in delicate
soft wind
spiraling, spiraling.

BACK STUDY

She lives,
emerging
from her marble chrysalis
receiving breath
from the stonecutter's hands,
her form revealed.

He speaks in stone
she answers in silence,
a seduction of light
and shadow.

AMERICAN LANDSCAPE:
A MOVEABLE POEM

Cottony clouds spin
shadows over the snowfields
of Mount Shasta concealing
for the moment
her mysteries.

In alpine pastures
silver-spoked irrigation wheels
circle in silence
like covered wagons at dusk.

Black and white cows
dominoes
on green felt
stack along
the snow-fed creek.

Hay bales square off
angled toward mortarless
century-old stone walls
tracing Shasta's circumference
in an unsolved
geometric equation.

ON THE OREGON COAST

I

An October mantra
of orange iridescence
brushes a haiku
onto the breath of evening.

II

Seagoing fishermen
loose earthly tethers
to walk upon water
and dream of big fish.

III

Black night
seafoam spreads
like magnolia skin
over cool wet sand.

PASSING THE SEASONS

I

The pewter blue Honda
whisks us from Oregon winter
to California spring
along the InterState —
a layer cake of blueberry sky
frosted by whipped clouds
mounds the peak of mystical Mt. Shasta,
home of the Atlantians
say the spiritually enlightened.

Frozen chocolate meadows metamorphose
into sherbet-green wheat whiskers.
Newborn lambs suckle ewes
sunbathing on warm pebbles
of a country road.
Snowfields retreat
to basted blue mountains
soon to wet fertile verdant valleys.

A yellow cropduster striped in black
banks toward earth,
to spew its venom
like an engorged hornet
then glides to the tank truck
for a refill in its
winged war on hungry insects —
their angel of death.

Flooded rice paddies
of Colusa, Williams, and Corning
pen haiku on parchment sky.

Soldierly rows of almond trees
in pink petal camouflage
highstep on yellow mustard.
Green hillocks, smooth as
woman's breasts
rise and fall like an inland ocean
nippled by seastacks of black and white cows.

II

A metal orchard of oil encased
in pastel-painted cannisters,
its towering cement branches belching
clouds of hydrocarbons over the freeway,
fouls water, earth and sky.
Cars converge on sinews of asphalt like
swarming armies of fire ants
gorging on farms and villages.

The Earth lies in wait.

QUIET CONVERSATION IN PALOUSE COUNTRY

My soul
      is transported
through this ancient land
sculpted long ago by natural forces.

Violent upheaval,
lava flows
great inland seas
      w i n d   s t o r m s
subdued Earth Mother here.

Upon her gently rounded bosom
perfectly traced patterns mimic
  ever-changing cloud formations
      in outline
of an artist's palette.

Swatch of sky
mixed with umber and ashen grey
      of rich volcanic soil
broken by patches of newly
germinated wheat.

A windmill, red barn and shimmering
grain silo accent the graceful flow
of tilled and untilled earth —
      a grand tapestry of
warp and weft directed
by Mother Nature's shuttle.

Unexpected patterns flicker upon the Earth
as light from the setting sun is re-directed

by the whimsy
of playful clouds

wresting

the shuttle from its course.

Simplicity reigns.

Sky

and

Earth

are

One.

Man's intrusion is not visible here.

EPIPHANY IN THE PARK

It was cold and rainy
as we left home
— my dog Bear and I —
the wood-handled umbrella
tucked under my arm,
the brown knit cap, pulled
low over the brows — January style.

But at the park
three blocks away
the blue-eyed sky encircled
the sun staged directly over
the grassy oval.
A gauzy-grey curtain of clouds
— from sky to Earth —
cut us off from all else
from whence we had come.

Plunged into warmth
in the island sauna, I discarded
my hat, coat and mittens
and we cavorted as children
of Earth dancing through the steam
rising from glistening cedar boughs
and scattered sapphires left
by raindrops as they melded with the sun.

A tidal wave of bliss
moved over us — in the eye
of the storm
the quiet

broken only
by voices on high
hidden in the cloud curtain
just feet away

the geese
in a single breath of motion
aerial calligraphy

order

      form

          simplicity

as quickly as ink dries,
they were gone.

We stood motionless
in reverence
then followed their sky tracks
back into January rain.

AMERICAN LANDSCAPE:
A SUNDAY MORNING AT BRITT GARDENS
11 August 1996

I

Strains of violins, cellos and violas
spring into the lapping cool of morning
bathing music lovers on the grassy hillside.
Champagne flutes teeter on picnic blankets
as unwelcome yellow stinged ones
flit from one offering to another.

Straw-hatted children
in Sunday best
shimmy up satin-skinned Madrones
absorbing Mozart their way.

The sun orbits in slow motion
its rays baton-like
conducting this idyllic respite
from the other world
of pre-election rhetoric
a seven-state power outage
the laborious search
for clues to an airline explosion.
Off in the distance
a grey veil stokes the arid valley
for another day of record heat.

II

Intermission

III

A golden harp en pointe
commands center stage
followed by its partner,
the delicate flute
en pirouette.
In duet, they recite Spenser's
Garden of Adonis
where souls are
reborn as flowers.
The bird-like flute
trills the transformation.

IV

Exit harp. Applause.
Enter piano, cello, violin.
Britt's ballet of musicians
suspend reality
create illusion
in this Spenserian garden for the soul.

DACHAU ON A SUNDAY AFTERNOON
14 July 1996

Dread builds
penetrates consciousness
like some unseen virus of the soul;
the stomach pushes upward
in revulsion unrelieved.

Suspended lifesize photographs
suspend reality for moments
while the body seeks balance
standing before the black and white
pit of mangled limbs, vacant
eye sockets, contorted grasping hands
unable to touch salvation.

T-shirt-clad youth point cameras
at the unthinkable
their hushed elders turn away
in confusion.
Death orders, body counts:
JewsCatholicsGermansPriests
ChildrenAustriansJewsGypsies
fuel unquenchable fires
in cast iron ovens whose
cavernous orifices
stand ready still.

Blistering bone-white pebbles,
stretching for acres where once
barracks stood, crunch
under sandal-footed pilgrims
shuffling to the hidden crematorium
in the grove of green trees

rooted in canals of blood
marked by rows of red-tissued begonias
whose beauteous innocence
riles the conscience.

The bullet-riddled wall
draws hesitant forefingers
to concave places.
Steepled memorials
CatholicProtestantRussianOrthodox
pierce the blue sky
in collective guilt
casting barbed shadows
over Dachau's skeletal remains.

OVERHEAD

ducks and geese soar
composing haiku in the sky

c e l e b r a t i n g
             c e l e b r a t i n g

their extended autumnal feast.

Do they know something
we don't know
or will winter wait awhile
content in the attention
of poets
and on the midnight hour

            s t r i k e!

BLIGHTED SPIRITS

Discarded toys
a pile of pink plastic
heaped before
the broken-screened cottage
flung aside by bored children
at summer's end
for banalities
of cartoon re-runs inside.
A deflated wading pool
drapes over the purple
and yellow tricycle
never to hold water again.

No favorite swimming hole
in the river.
No stack of grandfather's
building blocks for castles
to the sky.
No grandmother
in the front porch rocker
shelling peas.
No long rope swing in the maple tree.
No sandbox.
Disposable playthings
Disposable families
Disposable children.

FEBRUARY 16, 1996

She went at last
quietly
with more of a murmur
than a cry,
this mother of mine
whom I outlived
by twenty years
this day.

She birthed me
then deserted me
in my adolescence
teaching of Death
in my vitality,
left me a gift
the will to live
long past when
her genes dictated
her departure.

Her eyes grew hollow
her stomach swelled
not from a growing fetus
but with reckless cells
gorging like some
gluttonous creature
unable to leave its prey.

She worried about her four children
the youngest not yet five,
the eldest denying death
struggling to be free,

free from responsibility
free from siblings, free
from the stench of death.

"Your mother's gone to heaven,"
the father whispered,
"What am I to do?"
Anger engulfed the eldest
oozing sticky black
beneath every pore
seeking a vent
like oil,
unstoppable in its intensity
to disgorge from some dark cavern
in the underworld
but forced to flow
in subterranean seas
searching for centuries

                                        to be free.

RAPE OF A VIRGIN

I

the victim
stands

helpless

amidst her kin
threatened

dare she cry out?

her limbs grow weak
cold and clammy
he's reaching for the chains

spare me
she whispers
inaudibly

how barren
how abandoned
it has finally come to this
everywoman's fear

her green garment falls
the indignity stings
the violation

she stands
grappling
for balance
powerless
before her attacker

how best to meet
the inevitable?
she knows there were
others before her
but for her
it is the first time

his insatiable appetite
"relax and enjoy it"
NEVER!

Sap chokes her veins
her life seeps slowly away
images of fallen, naked
sisters lying prone
a violent shudder

accounts of others
left for dead
whose bony scattered
skeletons
the only markers
void of epitaphs

more lashes
the cold blade
pressing against her skin
assures submission

she feels the intrusion
inch by inch

her spirit readies
for release
despite an ignoble end.

II

the driver shifts into a
lower gear

"damn!" he thinks
"this is one big mutha
what a babe she
musta been in her day
funny, you'd think somebody'd
call a halt to things like this"

but he couldn't think about it
someone had to do it
pick up the remains
he had his family to support
didn't he?
besides
she probably
asked for it

i don't want to grapple
with it
leave it for the
bleeding heart
social workers
the politicians

still
it doesn't seem right

today it is harder than usual
her stature and nobility
make her harder to ignore

he'll make a few bucks off her
and so will the next guy
cuttin' and boxin' her up
trying to forget she had been alive

wonder where she'll end up
who'll claim her

probably
the weyerhaeusers
or georgia what's her name
or the guy from boise

Joyce Kilmer weeps.

SEASCAPE

The rain
distillation of clouds
gurgling tin-like
in gathering gutters,

sidles down in
silver slivers
drawing dream-like veils
across Monterey pines.

Liquid beads line up
on slats of deck chairs,
an abacus
counting quietly
time.

wayne

              impassioned fingers
      unfolded from his tightly clinched fists
              in slow motion
to lie flat   upon the table.

His drama was born!

        (his voice! oh God! his voice! Everyman's.)

Eyes, quickened hearts, labored breaths, undulating stom-
achs,
      but most of all — hearts — enfolded him.

In the room silence thickened. Love quietly slid down chairs,
      padded across the grey carpet and crawled hesitantly
      into his lap.

Morphine drips, velvet robes, questions unasked then asked,
      touching from across the room, revulsion, tears,
      laughter — we were one.

His affliction is now our affliction. Totally
      Welcomed — It can no longer consume him.
      Ever —
      It has been dissipated by all whom he touches
      with his voice. oh God! his voice.

We plead collectively to share it with him
      with our eyes.

It has left him, distributed equally
      in innocuous doses to everyone in the room.

      Our brother — Ourselves — Free

ABOUT THE POETS

JOYCE EPSTEIN, born in New York City, honed her skills on the monthly pages of '47, *the Magazine of the Year*. Moving to Los Angeles in 1948 she raised three children, wrote poetry, worked in the film industry for a Beverly Hills agency, later in advertising. Retiring to Ashland, Oregon in 1988, Joyce resumed her dormant career in PR and as poet and freelance writer. Her work has been dramatized by college and university Theatre Arts Departments and she is the author of the chapbook, *A Journey Through Life Unguarded*. Her poetry, essays and profiles have appeared in local and regional publications and in *CreativeCollection*, an anthology of Southern California writers. Her themes reference the common ground of journey and memory, of history as possibility.

SARA JAMESON came to Oregon in 1973 from Washington, D.C., reviving family roots of her great-grandfather who homesteaded briefly in the 1850s and her mother who was born in Portland. A poet, photographer, book reviewer, freelance writer and bookseller, she has published in magazines and newspapers including *Publishers Weekly*, *Reader's Digest*, the *Sunday Oregonian*, the *San Francisco Chronicle*, the *Bloomsbury Review* and *Fireweed*. She was poetry editor of *Southern Oregon Currents* from 1989 to 1991. Her poetry has appeared in *West Wind Review*, *Rogue's Gallery* and *KSOR Guide to the Arts* (now *Jefferson Monthly*). The moon is a frequent inspiration as are rocks and rivers. Family portraits form another major theme. She lives in Grants Pass, Oregon with her husband, elderly mother, and cat.

PATRICIA PARISH KUHN was born in Walla Walla, Washington, and has lived in the Pacific Northwest most of her life. Her poetry has appeared in several literary journals and has been selected for performance by the Drama Departments of Southern Oregon State College and the University of Portland. For five years she served as PR director and also assisted with planning for the Rogue Valley Writer's Conference at Southern Oregon State College. Many of her poems focus on the fragility of the earth and the disappearance of forests in the Northwest as well as on the human condition. She has given readings throughout Southern Oregon. Her work includes editing and writing for national travel guides; a travel column for a community newspaper as well as historical articles for state and regional publications. Patricia and her husband Richard have two grown children and live in Medford, Oregon.